PICKLES AND TARTS

PICKLES AND TARTS

MARIO SAVIONI

Chapter 1

Frank finished the story. It was sunny in the courtyard between boutique restaurants, a bakery, and Peet's Coffee. The weather was cooling in the shade. He was relaxed and comfortable. He could see through a screen door a woman working with flour in the back of the bakery. The woman reminded him of Nicole, who would be starting her life working in a field that would never make money. What made Frank think of this was working in the restaurant business, how an ex, a pastry chef, worked long hours filling measuring cups to add to pastry recipes, and how beautiful she was in her white outfit. She made about $13 an hour and lived in a house in the back of another house. Her home looked like a large chicken coop with a shower as small as the standing area in an airplane restroom. The three women, his ex, this woman in the bakery's back, and Nicole, were svelte and thin-faced. They had straight, strawberry blonde, and light brown hair. Frank could see the three of them with their hair pulled back in a ponytail. Nicole was young and probably starting at work. He knew if she began a job like a baker's, she couldn't afford it. He knew this too, coming to the end of his life, that life costs more than it seemed and that you had to sacrifice if you wanted to make it. Sacrificing also spoke of having to pick a line of work that you didn't particularly like. Still, it would give you an income to buy a house and another.

You couldn't stop until you had enough money for the rest of your life.

Frank contemplated his life, work, cafes, and short trips to San Francisco via BART to merely walk around and buy a meal that sometimes cost over $100. He imagined how much more it would cost if he weren't working and only traveled in the three cities: Oakland, San Francisco, and Walnut Creek. He wanted to travel abroad.

Frank had eaten, read, and slept earlier, and now he was staring into space as various people were walking by, catching the yellow leaves that littered the ground and moving them ever so slightly. Just off the curb's edge was moisture from the rain over the past few days. It was still gray overhead as scattered clouds blocked a sunny blue sky.

Nicole was 19 and had a smile that indicated terror and derision. Frank thought this was because his architecture professor said you could read people's faces by isolating quadrants: Each eye and each half of the mouth. When you did this, you could surmise their personalities based on words that came to you. The professor said we could have predicted Hitler and serial killers using this method. Frank saw terror and derision when he did this to Nicole's picture.

Chapter 2

Frank held up his hand and made a circle with his index finger and thumb, an "OK" sign, and enclosed Nicole's left eye. Her long, strawberry blonde hair, wispy, fell at angles on the faux leather jacket that covered her denim button-down blouse. Her brown eyes were fully open with the joy of childhood innocence, piercingly sure. She was aware of every movement.

There is a picture of Nicole where she is sticking her finger in her mouth and feigning vomiting. She is slightly behind a young Asian woman who is calm. The woman's hair is straight and long. She has a round face and a chubby upper arm and wears a black cocktail dress. It is sleeveless. The neckline covers her cleavage. It is made of open space in the weave about an inch across. She has a thin necklace with a diamond pendant that dips just below the top of her hem. Nicole's left hand is on the Asian woman's shoulder. Her hand is bright white against the Asian's tanned skin. Nicole's hand covers a lock of hair that goes under it and down the Asian woman's right arm. The Asian woman is wearing a white wristwatch and is carrying a white iPhone in her left hand. She slumps slightly toward Nicole and may not see Nicole's finger in Nicole's mouth, and Nicole blinks her eyes.

In another picture, she is too far away to get a good look
 at her. She is standing in a black and silver cocktail dress
with a thin neckline and tiny straps that rise from a small
"v" at the hem of her cleavage. The hem draws across
her chest and under her armpits. There are muted lines
and circles and a sheen to the material. Her dress rests
about five inches from her knees, and she is wearing a
pair of open-toed black high-heel shoes, sharply pointed,
with a single thin strap wrapped high around her ankle.

Frank studied the picture even more. He liked that
Nicole's calves were long, narrow, and slightly muscular.
He wanted fit, petite women.

Nicole's curvature is minimal. You could drop your
hands down her figure and barely move left or right as
you went down. In the photo, she is jutting her hips
forward with her hair pulled back. A woman, maybe her
mother, is on her right. They all possess a slightly
squinting left eye when they smile. Her mother looks like
she is in her late 30s, maybe early 40s. She is also
wearing a cocktail dress, except hers is all black. The
hem moves across her chest as a long arch from shoulder
to shoulder. The straps on her shoulders are about an
inch wide.

Two males in the photograph have an early 20-year-old
"future Wall Street Trader" look: Frat boys with big
smiles. The one holding Nicole and her mother pushes

his chest out of his tuxedo jacket. Nicole appears recessive between the boys and her mother, willing to allow them their feigned dominance against the person holding the camera. Perhaps the photographer is her father. She almost seems angelic, younger, and less confident than when she had her arm around her female friend in the previous picture. They are standing on a brick walkway intersecting a small, gray rock path. Green grass moves from the walkway to a wooden fence fifty yards out, covered in manicured bushes. The backyard is lush. All the plants are deep green.

The image is an arm and a fraction of the seat, a section of a barbecue, and tall trees filling the sky. Frank guessed that the photo depicted Danville.

Chapter 3

Frank closed his eyes and pictured Nicole. He wanted to get closer, to smell her mouth, to draw his tongue across her teeth and run his fingers through her hair. Frank imagined how she might smell, but however she smelled, it didn't matter. He only knew that she would be fresh to him. It was long ago that Frank felt comfortable with his mouth. No matter how often he brushed his teeth, he could taste the thousands of meals he had eaten. Age gave him a sense of uncleanliness. Nicole smiled at him, but he knew it wasn't for him. It was just a picture. She was smiling for someone, a girlfriend, a lover, her parents, but not the fifty-four-year-old.

Frank was bald, physically in shape because he rode his bike up Mt. Diablo, but not as often as he liked, but probably more often than he would if he were younger. There were days in his youth when he surfed in the sun for over six hours. Perhaps Frank was buffer then. Besides the biking, he would do about five pull-ups with his separated shoulder, torn rotator cuff, tennis elbow, and usually around twenty-five push-ups and fifty crunches. These greatly tired him, and he could barely get out of bed each morning. His right hip ached. It wasn't appendicitis, his doctor told him. It was probably muscular, but the doctor ran a CT scan and found diverticulitis.

Frank closed his laptop and wondered where Nicole was and what she thought. Did she have the exact needs? Of course, Nicole did. She got them met by her boyfriend, and maybe she was even partially interested in other boys, but Frank was a distraction, perhaps a mistake to her.

Chapter 4

A few weeks ago, Frank was on *Spark*'s dating site and selected Nicole's picture. She must have chosen him because they were both notified of a match.

It surprised Frank; she was lovely but very young, thirty-six years younger. He didn't know what to say. Too often on *Spark*, he'd pushed the green button when he saw these cute but much younger women, and usually, if they matched, they would promptly send an invite for a girlfriend experience or a "GFE." Not only was he unwilling to pay for sex that was not mutual, but the act of engaging for money was also incriminating. It was bad enough that he had a clue that his advances were unlikely supported, if not by the young woman herself, then certainly not by the community. Her friends would not accept the romantic affections of the two, who were so different in age.

Despite their age difference, Frank was still interested in communicating. He saw this as a chance to pursue the inevitable rejection of society, but he needed to experience it for himself.

Frank said briefly about how she looked like someone who had read the Brontes. After reading about Charlotte Bronte's life in Michael Schmidt's *The Life of the Novel*,

Frank felt like an authority.

"What is Brontes even?" Nicole wrote.

What this said was that she probably wasn't a prostitute. Nicole's response was innocent, plus a prostitute would have already sent him a link to another page indicating a girlfriend experience (GFE). It seemed like she was a nineteen-year-old girl unexposed to the Brontes. He figured, or hoped she had since it seemed to represent what a young, intellectual female would feel compelled to read besides the Brontes were young when they crafted their masterpieces; Charlotte was 31, for example, when she published *Jane Eyre*.

Chapter 5

Nicole could be a man, Frank also thought, but this was *Spark*, based on *Visage*, so the chances of her being someone other than she claimed seemed unlikely, but then the GFEs were also uncertain. It also told him that she probably wasn't interested in looking up the word.

Frank could imagine her, given the four or five pictures, and what this response indicated was a smile and a carefree, even quiet, reaction. Perhaps she was being cocky. He imagined the same response might await him if he saw her in public. Nicole would respond, "Who is this guy?" and "What is he doing talking to me?"

Frank could imagine her sleek, unbroken line of youthful flesh as she sat beside him: Forced, awkward. She laughed when he said they should talk: "What should we talk about?"

"I guess you're correct," Frank said. "It's fairly obvious I am attracted to you." He dared not look into her eyes, controlling his head. The truth was obvious. He could relate to almost nothing except wanting to write about this.

Nicole looked over her shoulder at Frank, who was sitting on the couch, "Who is Brontes even?"

"*Jane Eyre* writer," Frank said, "Amy, Charlotte, and

Emily were sisters who wrote. I know you've at least tried to read one."

"Nope, I haven't," Nicole said. Her shortness, her certainty, spoke of her investment in the conversation. He could feel the futility in his having started it. He studied the words, something he could say. The space was both expansive in possibility but also limiting and obvious. He tended toward the negative, and the word "nope" was staring at him, almost like it was another hint of the predictable outcome, but he chose to ignore it.

Chapter 6

"Hello again Nicole," he wrote. "I haven't read the books either." He starts to think of this experience as an expression of truth and see if he can connect with her based on his reality and be open in his responses.

"I am currently reading *The History of the Novel*, and I happened on the section," Frank typed, "where Schmidt talks about the Brontes' influence. Beyond that, it feels weird contacting you because I realize you are much younger. I just saw your picture, and as an artist, I thought you were beautiful. I wondered what you thought and was flattered that you would respond to me, causing a match. Perhaps you mistakenly moved my photo to the right instead of to the left."

Frank stopped and looked at his keyboard momentarily, giving his mind a chance to catch up.

"Also, as a writer," Frank said, "I thought it might be interesting to flesh this out by exploring how we both feel and think about the other and turn it into a short story. I don't know what your intentions are. What would you like to happen? Do you want to meet for coffee? Do you want to work on an article? What is on your mind? What do you need? I look forward to hearing from you again."

Chapter 7

The cafe had graphic paintings: reds, greens, pinks, yellows, triangles, lines, circles, a heart in the middle of one of the paintings, a movement toward the center where these forms, painted with thick lines. A loud, brassy meringue came from the speakers. You couldn't help but be affected by it. Before he realized it, Frank was tapping his foot. Then, he looked around the room to see if anyone noticed. Frank saw an Asian woman on her computer on the right. He wondered if she saw him, just as it seemed that she was thinking about him, but maybe it was his imagination. She was attractive and young. She was sitting with a man wearing earbuds connected to a phone. He was Asian too. They wore running shoes, three white stripes, and a black and gray background. They matched the stripes going down the length of his long-sleeved gray sweatshirt. His socks were red, black, and white. Her feet were together as he scratched the back of his neck. She wore a dark gray jacket with a fur-edged hood. Her black-brown hair poured over her hood. Her mouth was open, and she wore earbuds too. It was a cold night. They sat sipping tea and looking at their respective computer screens.

By this time, Frank conceded to his limited reading. He was only glancing at, not even comprehending, the books he referenced as his means to a Master of Fine Arts

(MFA) education or at least to prepare for the Graduate Record Exam (GRE) about which he was afraid. The GRE was a line not crossed in his lifetime. He was not good at standardized tests, and he reasoned that studying for the GRE or Law School Admissions Test (LSAT) would require altering his personality to do well enough to get into the school of his choice.

"Beyond that," Frank wrote, "it feels weird contacting you because I saw your picture, and as an artist, I thought you were a beauty." This statement belied that while Frank did indeed think Nicole was a beauty, he thought of her sexually. Her face was "perfect." There was no noise with the issue of her complexion. Other photos of her were of an innocent and kind person. One showed her with two men her age. He asked her why she chose him.

Frank was hoping she was attracted. However, he prefaced with "As a writer" to offer her an alternative, which would save his face if she accidentally selected him. If it had been an accident, the rest of her interaction for a short story could have been fabricated. It had to be "true," and thus, he hoped her response would be something more interesting than if she merely had made a mistake.

Frank had made many mistakes on the site, and luckily,

at those times, the other people weren't interested. He never had to tell them that he wasn't interested. He also asked her what she needed because he had read this somewhere to ask a person. The word 'need' embodied a direct question, cutting out the possibility for misunderstanding and the passage of emotional baggage. He hoped it would open a range of responses. He wanted to meet her in person to see if she existed. That meeting would remove the uncertainty.

"Hahaha, this is so unique!" she said. "You're a writer then? I love to write. It's funny you mention writing a short story. I am currently taking a short story class focused on analyzing character development. I swiped right to do something spontaneous. I'm not looking for a romantic partner. I have a boyfriend. It's fun to talk to different people sometimes. Right?"

Chapter 8

Frank felt relieved. She opened the door to further their communication. Her taking a course on character development was a coincidence. She "Swiped right to do something spontaneous." At least she was up for an exciting interaction, but she qualified her engagement: "I have a boyfriend; I am not looking for a romantic partner."

Frank thought about this. Was he looking for a partner or someone with whom to have sex? He did not think beyond that simple, single transaction -- the satisfaction of his baser needs, not realizing that his needs might go on given the possibility of this opportunity and mutual attraction.

Nicole added innocently, "It's fun to talk to different people sometimes."

In this, Frank thought that, yes, it was fun to talk to different people, but in doing so, there was also the question of underlying motivation. He was taking chances in communicating with someone he would otherwise be afraid to engage in person. The potential was a sandwich of rejection. He already knew that society would not support his interests. His unmet need was sex, but his attraction required someone beautiful.

He couldn't help this. Even with his attractive past partners, he could not get satisfaction. He was not getting laid correlated to his sense of accomplishment in life, to the fact of his tiny dick, how she smelled, how he smelled if he had a loss for words when they conversed. All of his lovers eventually left him. He could not hold on. He didn't know what to say. He had no friends, and he obsessed over his past lovers as if they were the works in a gallery, a series of lines connected to his longing. They were shapes, sounds, and ideas that he looked at, listened to, and contemplated. His relationships seemed like the affirmation of an agreement to allow obsession, which would eventually turn creepy. None of them were in his life at this time.

Frank went for years until he would eventually capture one. These innocent birds looking for freedom, you might think, ultimately, he went for it. Cheating girlfriends, angry spouses who wanted out, and even someone needing a green card all seemed damaged. As he got older, these affairs grew less and less, and the last time he made love to someone he was interested in and thus not sickened by was about 13 years ago. His reaching Nicole and continuing their conversation without, of course, their meeting seemed hopeful. That's where he was in his pathetic life. Yes, there was other evidence of a disinclination, and he had even changed the conversation to one involving writing a short story together.

Frank worked on that part of it promising to get back to her so that she might grant him the response he wanted. He worked carefully, and the days went by as he crafted the piece, looking out of his sliding glass door onto the apartment complex approximately 75 yards from his balcony, which looked out over a pool. Frank had a cold, dressed in a gray top and bottom sweatsuit with a hood and slippers. They were black Crocs-like in design with a soft black fur lining. Underneath the sweatshirt were layers of black long-sleeved shirts, one of which was a female long-john he'd bought at REI on sale. Although it was a lady's large, it was tight on him, and the cuffs never went to his wrists. He had to pull at them. The shirt helped him during the winters in California when he was never quite warm enough and would get sick, sometimes four times a year. He used to think it was because he was allergic to wheat, but even when Frank wasn't eating it, he still got a cold or the flu. He would submit easily and lay in bed for days. When sick, Frank was miserable, which embarrassed him. He wasn't a man's man. He took his body seriously, like a woman might, listening to every emotional nuance.

Chapter 9

It was sunny outside, and the sky was relatively blue, except Frank could see the light gray cloud cover, and he knew, having learned the lesson after arriving from Honolulu in 1993, that just because the sun was out, it didn't mean that it was warm outside. Frank looked down at the words Nicole had sent, and he looked up too at the reality that they both must be aware. In Frank's mind, he was hopeful.

"That's fabulous," Frank said, "I was talking about a short story built out of this experience. It felt weird having a physical attraction to you, but it also appears that we both have an interest in writing unless this is a class you have to take."

"Well," Nicole said, "if you were to write a short story about this meeting, what would you say? And no, this class is an option. I decided to take it."

In Frank's eyes, Nicole was flitting about the issue that most concerned him. Still, he was either ignorant that she had answered the question about her sexual interest in that there wasn't one, or he dismissed it and fed off the contact she was giving. His desires were more potent than his better judgment.

"I think," Frank said, "that we've already said a lot: The implication of your short responses and then your grand explosion of statements, where you could finally relate, you were spontaneous. What was on your mind when you leaped? That is what is interesting. By pressing the green button when I saw you, perhaps the same spontaneity is not. The short story, I would say, is to put our words into quotes, going back and forth and filling in the blanks in the conversation. There were intentions on both sides of our conversation."

"A short story," Frank continued, "gets at those intending to inform. It's been a theme with me of late. I told my friend Lani that I felt like a dirty older man now that I've gotten older, but my tastes in women have remained the same. As an artist, perhaps as the son of a television model, I can't help but find impossibly beautiful women attractive. That would be something I might explore. What about you? What would you say? I pictured you laughing at my absurdity of trying to maintain a conversation. It must have felt trying. Was it uncomfortable? 'Why is this guy writing?' you may have thought. 'Is he crazy? I was kidding. I've got a boyfriend. Doesn't he know this?'"

Chapter 10

When Nicole reminded him of this, he knew the stupidity of his attraction. Turning this into a short story was, in effect, a kind of fetishizing of what he realized he could never have. The short story represents the shoe that would never fit, even though Frank may have come upon it. He was in his room some unknown distance from her should have told him that the relationship wasn't real. She was playing with him, even though she might have sensed he was an average person, and although entirely not her type, she sensed his humanity and didn't want nor feel the need to hurt him. She was curious about what was happening. Frank hoped she had some daddy issue to work on, but their intentions were unaligned. Missing a father does not correlate to wanting sex with an older man. She might have wanted to feel protected but not engaged in intercourse unless she had been, and that was another thing entirely. Molested women had come to him in the past, and sex was on the menu, but so was their desire to control the sex, whereas Frank was only interested in having it.

Frank picked up a clear glass mug of hot fresh vegetable soup that he had just made to clear his congestion. He raised it to his mouth just as the neighbor across the way was walking. She was too far away for Frank to understand her figure or how she looked. Neighbors from that unit and the other one to its right came and went at least every three months. He had only seen her about three or four times for a month or two. She came out again wearing a black coat that went to her waist and a magenta T-shirt with white letters underneath. She seemed tall and large-boned. She wore black-rimmed glasses. She left her door open and went down the steps again. She was returning with things in her arms. Each time, it would appear that she knew he was looking at her, but he couldn't tell she knew he was there simply because it was dark inside his apartment, the window shut, and there might have been a reflection on the sliding glass door. He couldn't see into her apartment. Her door behind the screen was open, although the overhang didn't cast a shadow over the door, wherein, in his case, his balcony was covered by the roof.

Frank finished the broth and looked at the vegetables that remained. Nearly the entire mug was full. He went to the kitchen, poured more broth and vegetables into the cup, and grabbed a small plate and spoon. He returned to his desk, and the neighbor's door remained open. It was cold outside. What was she saying? Or was he imagining her invitation? He returned to the short story and Nicole.

"A short story would set up the scene," he added, "It would describe *Spark* and go from there. It would represent the two people. You would have to do this because I don't know you. What is happening in your life? Who are you? What do you dream about becoming, etc.? People want to know. They like to relate to others with common threads. Then there is me. What was going through my head? Didn't I know it would be awkward? Wasn't it uncomfortable? Until you responded, I didn't realize I had nothing to say, and then by intellectualizing the conversation, I could shift all of it into this story. Perhaps it is just about me.

"Last night, I kept thinking I should just cut this off. It was risky. Still, as a writer attempting to garner some semblance of virtue, I am interested in getting to the truth—is it a simple attraction to beauty and youth? I am interested in your feelings. I know they are not romantic. How could they be? I can't sleep with someone for whom there is no attraction. How could you?"

"Anyway," Frank said, "the short story might start as:

"'Glenn saw Alexis' picture. He pressed the green button because he wanted to. Alexis was someone he wanted and didn't consider the other information that might have given him more. It was a dare. What would she think about him? He didn't know. He just pressed the icon, and her picture went right. He wanted. Then, and he can't remember this, she matched him. She said later that she only did it spontaneously. She said she wanted to make

friends with other people. For Glenn, it posed a problem. What would he say to her? He was attracted, but reality showed its face as he imagined her doing this on a whim and then laughing at the audacity. She was already in love with David, who would find this ridiculous. It could also anger him to know what Glenn was doing. She would tell Gretchen and Mimi, but she had yet to see them. Perhaps she could write this as a story for class - what she thought of him. What was he doing at this moment? Where was he? He thought of her too. They were having a conversation that meant they had to think about what was being said and about themselves, and it was risky, at least for Glenn. He felt embarrassed but also drawn to it. As mentioned, everything is about sex. For Glenn, it was more interesting than the sunlight over the neighborhood outside that seemed never to move except as the trees stirred faintly. Perhaps they would meet for coffee in some urban coffee shop or in the suburbs since they didn't know where the other lived. She imagined the awkwardness of his attraction and the hopelessness of translating his dreams into intellectualization. She just looked back at him almost as awkwardly as he felt. They talked about themselves and the story that was moving forward. It turned out that he was very attracted to her, and she was thinking about the story for class, her life, and the risks she would take for something to tell her friends.

"It was awkward, Mimi," Alexis told her friend. "He was wearing seersucker shorts and a blue and white striped shirt. He was so informal. I could feel his nervousness. I guess he realized how old I was, and it made him feel evil. I thought it would be fine, but I felt bad for him. I had no intention for any of this to happen, but there I was, looking at him. He was fidgeting with a Starbucks cup."

Chapter 11

"Wow!" Nicole said, "You've got a rough draft."

"I want to type it up and then think about what I need to do to flesh it out," Frank responded, "I'm going to think about what I felt when I wrote you and about the things that are happening. Today, for example, I opened a book I bought in July called *And Everyday It Was Overcast* by Paul Kwiatkowski, and this particular passage struck a chord with me:

He sold ecstasy, heroin, acid, and coke to punk high school kids. His house smelled like Vicks VapoRub. Over and over, I watched him single out the sad loner girls, get them addicted to opiates, and make them his until absolutely no one wanted them.

Frank cited this section of the book because the entire book appealed to him. He was interested in the young girls and days of youth, where he remembered how easy it was to attract and seduce. He was also drawn to the pictures from the book because they haunted him. The kids were drugged and isolated in a backwoods area. Excursions into drug-taking and sexual frivolity saddened him for the advantage the boys and men were taking of the girls—how one older woman was indeed so awkward and thin in her pictures that it didn't seem like she would ever survive.

Nicole said, "I would hate to have that happen to me. Although I am talking to you, for example, and I get that you are a normal person, I understand how someone lost could be taken by someone they needed to trust. But I also know when it starts to feel uncomfortable, and I know I could tell that guy would take advantage of me, and it's not cool!" She was looking down at the screen, and she could feel the predicament that the "Sad, loner girls" were getting. It pissed her off. She looked up from her computer and looked around her bedroom. Everything was in its place; her family was in the other rooms, and her father worked. She felt safe. She didn't have to go outside of her home to find safety.

The computer made a doorbell sound, and Frank looked up at the red medallion at the top right with all the other icons, making him smile.

Another *bong* rang out with another statement by Nicole: "When I was younger, I met this guy in our neighborhood. He was lanky and somewhat cute, and we messed around. I remember him lifting my shirt, putting his hands on my stomach, and moving under my bra. We kissed a lot, and he also touched me, you know where. I don't remember what happened after that. The next thing I knew, he was the kid in High School with the drugs. He had a lot of girls following him around, and I think they used to party at his parent's house. He and his group were popular, but they also seemed strung out, with an edge to them. I thought, I never wanted to be like that. I didn't see the point."

Chapter 12

This struck Frank, and it caused him to go back in time when he was a ten-year-old living in Hawaii. He told his friend Taki he was attracted to a Filipino girl they danced with during the May Day Parade at Jefferson Elementary School in Waikiki. The next thing he knew, Taki asked him to meet him outside class, and Taki threatened him that if Frank ever tried to date her, he would punch him. Frank was the smallest boy in class. Taki was the second smallest. Still, Taki greatly intimidated Frank. Then, in sixth grade, Kazu and the other boys would throw a hard plastic ball at him in a game called 'Bean 'em and Run.' Instead of chasing the other boys, they kept throwing the ball at Frank. Eventually, he realized he wasn't their friend, the Haole, the outsider.

He went to Noelani Nishiki's with Caitlin Watanabe, his "girlfriend" at the time. They held hands, walked home, and that was about it. A Samoan classmate escorted him outside near one of the only bushes between the classroom and the Ala Wai Canal and threatened to kill him if he ever saw him with Caitlin again. It turned out that the Samoan was later in jail for murder. What upset him in these cases was that neither Taki nor the Samoan seemed to contact the girls. Were they jealous? Frank wondered. Then, in intermediate school, Frank managed to tell Taki that he liked Sara, and then Taki and Kazu tricked him into meeting them by the tennis court. Frank can't remember who punched him in the stomach first, but it made him cry primarily because of the injustice: It didn't seem to matter what Sara thought or if she even knew. He never sat with them on the bench again, not to be made a fool. Frank did, however, dance with another Caitlin during a dance period at school. He, Caitlin, and another couple were the only people on the dance floor. The effect on Frank was to take away that part of his childhood. He reasoned that this may have been the cause for his attraction to Nicole. He also knew that he was attracted to women and that their ages didn't matter. Nicole was beautiful to him despite probably being considered beautiful to anyone.

Chapter 13

There was a sense of compliance by the women in the book *And Everyday It Was Overcast*. Sexual favors were probably not even on their minds because they wanted drugs, distraction, and excessiveness due to some greater or different need that seemed to have very little to do with sex. Frank could not imagine himself drugging a woman to get what he wanted. Such an action would destroy the relationship itself. Frank's sexual experiences in the past weren't romantic or intimate. They were sloppy and stressful. By morning, he considered the possibility of having impregnated the woman or contracting some disease. In his sexual liaisons, he was irresponsible.

Frank also recalled a *Human Talk* post to *Visage* called "What teens want to know about sex," where it said, "pleasure can't be done in a vacuum." What it reinforced for Frank was that circumstances and the environment contextualized relationships. If there ever was any, Nicole's interest in him had to come from something she was either compensating for or perhaps out of some dark interest she was following. The talk also asked why sex was so good. Frank looked upon Nicole as sublime; her figure and face aroused him from what he could tell. Beauty is powerful, he thought.

"Otherwise, writing a good short story considers the

events and ideas in peoples' minds," Frank wrote to Nicole. He couldn't get her out of his mind. "Readers aren't going to believe something that isn't steeped in contemporary culture. I am also interested in the age difference between us and how we might bridge that. I feel the coincidence of you taking the literature class constructed a bridge. Maybe you want to be a writer, too. I don't know if you know about the television program *Californication*. David Duchovny sleeps with an underage woman, and he writes a novel about it, and she ends up taking it and publishing it. He concedes it to her because she blackmails him. She gets famous for it and travels doing book appearances. I want to do a story that explores social media, *Spark*, etc. I need you to express yourself. How does all of this make you feel? What do you think? What do you want to say? It also explores the idea that a fifty-four-year-old man has your attention. Do I? Am I deluding myself? Do you want to work on the story to submit to your writing class? As I was saying, perhaps we could write it together. Write your reactions down. We could write a novelette. See Bolaño's new book at the bookstore or look for it online."

"Writing is about telling the truth," Frank said. "People want to know about us and what goes on. What do you think of this?" he added.

"As for what I need from you, just the truth," Frank

said. "I looked back and saw that you like to write. You've also said that you had a boyfriend, which was all spontaneous. Tell me about that. What did you think when you saw me and when you pushed the green button? I mentioned what I would write about myself. I am being completely open. I've told you that I liked you. What would you tell your boyfriend, mother, father, and friends?

"Now that I can look back at the conversation, it runs like a dialog between two people. What is missing are feelings we have that we aren't putting down. That makes a short story: The dialog between characters and the context and feeling. What they feel becomes the outcome, as it does in real life. People start to share themselves and take risks, and the other starts caring. There is a humanity that develops. They treat themselves how they want to treat others, but is this intention always looming in the background that colors their conversation and actions? It is amazing what people do to achieve intimacy, to connect. That connection means something in the end. It is what we remember about life and what was most important."

"To eat pickles and tarts, of course," Nicole said.

This response startled Frank. The sexual innuendo was apparent. "Pickles" for men and "Tarts" for the young woman she was, and to eat them implied a phantasmagoric mutual union, which, of course, was what he wanted, and then for her to cooperate in the intention both tantalized him and made him nervous. Perhaps she was playing with him, and as long as they were just doing this in cyberspace, it wasn't real anyway. The game was continuing.

Chapter 14

Frank responded to her: "I assume this is an answer to the questions about what you tell your boyfriend, mother, father, and friends. I read an article yesterday about how a man making time on the Internet was trying to pick up an underage girl. Someone contacted the police. He said something lewd, and he was drawn in and arrested. Any parent or boyfriend wouldn't want their loved one predated. I question my motives, thinking of Wilhelm Stekel's *Sexual Aberrations*: 'He is a Don Juan without having to sin. The female appears to him devoid of any fascination because the seductive qualities have been violently passed to a smaller object, the rose. It is no sin to kiss roses. Nor can the rose put his potency to the test.'"

Her response touched Frank. It made him warm inside and hopeful. Maybe Nicole was interested in the sexual play that he was inclined to want, and she seemed so aware, playful, and sarcastic. Therefore it reminded him that IQ was present early, and awareness of ulterior motives could be felt and understood certainly by nineteen, which is what Nicole was. Still, he saw another side of her. She was even brighter than he imagined, and she was clearly in control.

"You would tell the family and your boyfriend to eat

pickles and tarts," Frank said. "Intelligence is apparent early. If you are as you say (nineteen), your brain is where it will be, which does not explain your motivations, intent, or your experience. I told an editor-friend about you, and he drew his hands in the air, comparing maturation levels. He assumes we'll have nothing to say. We live in different worlds. I agree with him in the sense your intentions are not mine. Our conversation is just a game for you: The batting about of an indefensible mouse by a cat. For me, it is the churning of emotions and desires, hopes and dreams, and perhaps a death march. 'In the very middle of the court was a table with a large dish of tarts upon it: they looked so good that it made Alice quite hungry to look at them -- "I wish they'd get the trial done," she thought, "and hand round the refreshments!" There seemed to be no chance of this, so she began looking at everything about her to pass away the time.'"

"When my friend spread his hands," Frank said, "I wanted to hug him. I exploded with compliments. It reminded me of why we were friends. He is brilliant and nonjudgmental, and so many other people I have known are negative and whiny. I knew the lack of commonality would be a problem. What would we talk about except the truth, which would be both linguistic and visceral? Any relationship is about the truth, expressed openly or condemned to silent, nonverbal remarks. I refused to be miserable in this. I would tell her everything, hoping she would do the same. Why else would two people be so engaged?"

The question remained, Frank thought, why was she in on this? Was it an experiment, was he a potential sugar daddy, or was she real? Was she interested in what I had to say? Was she just interested in this man, who was interested in someone much younger, at least on paper?"

The conversation would go on, it seemed, just as they all had until she knew the truth. Her lines were so short as to be without a trace of gender or investment that soon enough, if she didn't bite, Frank would cut it, which would be the story. After all, the reader wants the truth. They might also hope that this led to something.

Nicole was quiet on her end. He could only imagine what she might be doing or thinking.

Chapter 15

He imagined eating tarts, as she so snidely stated. He wanted all of her, her fragility, her cockiness, her shyness, her discovery after being seduced, and the loneliness she would feel. But he also knew he was deluding himself. He wasn't in control. She was. She wasn't interested in him, and that's where he lost his power. He could be as honest and forthcoming as he wanted, but he could not persuade her.

No, Frank did not control Nicole. She talked to Frank as if in a "chatroom," and she could easily dismiss him with a button.

Frank deluded himself into thinking that he could keep the conversation going if he just continued to be honest and tried not to wield power over her. She was more intelligent than he was. His desires were blatant and visible. She knew what he wanted.

Perhaps Frank was willing to destroy his power and freedom to be with her. Is that how powerful her beauty was? In reality, Frank deluded himself into believing that they were both seeking acceptance and love. Elliot Perlman called it the long journey to love: "Fetishes are about the search for love." How better to find it, Frank thought, in putting themselves out there and being treated well?

No matter their age difference, Frank thought Nicole was perfect, and Frank meant something to her -- a rite of passage into her feminine power?

Frank's condo was white and spare: A white Ikea chair in his living room advertised in a Skinnerian box that gets pushed like a mechanical dildo over and over and a desk. There were two tall and thin speakers, two bookshelves, his mother's silver, a table he made, white, organic-shaped, and the Ikea twin mattress on the floor with unheard-of thread count white-cotton sheets and a pillow. When he saw her, the condo was finally clean of everything except the essentials. Frank was only interested in experiencing this and writing about it. He wanted intimacy and genuine friendship, and most of all, he wanted to know what she thought and why, but he was lost.

Frank imagined that they would lie together on a bed talking for hours, and they would touch each other. That touching would send electrical charges to his brain, but he would not do what he did not feel was welcome.

Frank imagined further that they would lay on the bed like two self-administering psychological patients. His resisting and her being open was their friendship, and only in this trust and discipline could they be together, or else any wrong move or word would send them spiraling out of control in defensive positions. He remembered this from many one-night stands. A relationship, he thought, is what it is. The truth is always there, waiting, watching, and wondering when one or both of them got tired of lying. Frank felt the situation had revealed the truth.

Frank came to an understanding of why he was so interested in her despite the obvious attraction. When he was ten, he moved to Honolulu after his father died. It was just him, his mother, and his sister. He had at least two sexual meetings, one with a babysitter, who was eighteen, gorgeous, who had spread her legs for him and he wanted to play doctor, and the other, a neighbor, spread her legs in an ivy cave in a lot at the end of the block. That all evaporated with his father's death, and his confidence suffocated like a snuffed candle.

"'Father Figure Seeks Daddy's Little Girl' to be loved by someone beautiful and innocent since there is innocence in the attraction that always remains veiled."

Frank thought of this for a Craigslist ad if his conversation with Nicole got no further.

Frank told himself that the most important thing to learn from their cyber conversation was that she lived in a different world. You've done something too, he thought with her in mind, "Accidents," we call them, were "spontaneous" means "accidentally," and for her, "unique" meant that she was hoping you didn't take her mistake as an invite because she was clear that she had a boyfriend.

Infatuation and dreams are like this; Frank kept thinking. They do not live in reality. She wants nothing to do with you. Her brevity, although pithy, proves that. She comes to your long, drawn-out responses not to spend much time but also not to reveal your pathetic, hopeless attempts at seduction. Everyone can see your veiled prose and intellectualization for what it is. Sometimes it feels like forever when she writes again, and you apologize, but it has become creepy as if it wasn't before. You drip of desperation. You are a sewage pipe full of seeping longing. Her half-smile has become a cautionary silence, a joke that reveals your ailment.

Chapter 16

Nicole hands the portable computer to her friends, laughing at Frank. It's still too early for them to sense the sadness, but Nicole tells them it has been happening for days. "Watch this," she says, "how I write a single word, and he comes back with a myriad of interpretations, camouflaging his desire. Luckily, he hasn't said something about roses. Yes, this whole thing is a fetish. He is probably home in a dark room just waiting for me, and I ignore him."

"Alex says a man's fetish begins at a moment of conjoined anxiety and stimulation when, for some reason, the man is made to feel that if he expresses his sexuality at that precise moment, he will be breaking some rule, and love will be withheld from him," (Perlman).

"I know he is there; I can feel him," Nicole says, "Can't you? Don't you know men like this?"

"There was a scientist," Frank sends to Nicole, "Edward T. Hall, who described a box of rats. Two alpha rats would mate with all the female rats, and the female rats would coyly wait for them or follow them around.

Another hierarchy of male rats would try to mate with

one or two of the females, but they were not usually welcome. So, these second-tiered male rats took their shots when the alpha males weren't looking. There was another tier of male rats that cowered in the corners. They were quiet, almost invisible, and completely ignored.

"On occasion," Frank continued, "the female rats would find themselves ignored or bashed by the other females or left brokenhearted by the alpha males, and as they felt sorry for themselves, the cowering males saw an opportunity. Each time coitus was charitable or to cause jealousy, the females would allow themselves to be played with, touched, and penetrated by the lesser males. It never ended well for the more inferior males. The ostracization always began immediately when the female rat saw her mistake.

"Weakness and isolation were not good signs for the health of the brood," Frank continued as if Nicole were listening in her house in her room. "If the alpha males knew of the weakness, they would have ripped the outcast apart, except that even alpha males need their sleep. The conniving rat saw his chance and took it, hoping that the uniqueness of his circumstances would allow him what he wanted more than anything, but of course, these things never really happened unless they were rape or charity. Rejection always follows this, and honesty is the only way out.

"So, in this case," Frank said, "I told you every stop and reminded you often what my intentions were, and you saw it for the joke it was, a novelette, more like a novelty. I wrote instead of lived. You told your friends, thinking for a moment what was wrong. I even dared to say that my friend said our maturation levels were almost too far apart. We both know my maturation is childlike. I couldn't embrace the truth that you would never allow this chronological breach, and even if you did, society would not allow it. If we appeared in public, it would be a father and daughter. Otherwise, it was an indication of something wrong.

"I waited and wondered," Frank said, "and she cringed from what she had started."

Chapter 17

Nicole wrote back before he continued: "I haven't told them," she said, "that I am talking to you. They don't even know what *Spark* is. Why are you on *Spark*?"

"Well, as you might have guessed, under the veil of my intellectualizing," Frank said, "I want to be with someone who turns me on. I've written pages in a state of absurdity attempting to seduce you, knowing full well that even with reverse psychology or honesty, the truth of this is obvious. What could I ever hope would come of this? Nothing. I have settled for the process, and you've given me kindness. I see the wisdom of the female, who tries out of kindness to wake the dreamer. I hear you. You've been kind. Thank you. I want you to know I appreciate you. Such a lovely name, such a lovely person."

"Aw," Nicole said, "I like talking to you too! I love to meet new people. It has been a pleasure getting to know you. Do you hope to get married or have kids?"

"Nicole," Frank said, "you always surprise me. I write what I feel, listening to Damien Rice's 'My Favorite Faded Fantasy,' and it seems to say what I had hoped. He sings, 'What it all could be with you.' It is beautiful, and I had written him that since his split with Lisa Hannigan, he might never achieve the beauty they possessed when singing together. I was wrong; the cut is as radiant as light. I like talking to you as well. The pleasure is mine. I do hope to get married, but I do not want kids. You'll make a good mother, given how you find the good things in people. In your latest response, I may have what I need to complete the story. I will let you know when I finish. Thank you so much for listening. I have learned much from you, and I have gone through a passage in knowing myself."

"Show me the finished draft!" Nicole said, "I would love to read it. I am glad you have personally benefitted from our encounter."

"The word 'personally' is telling," Frank told her. "That is what this whole thing is. It is about me. None of this has been valuable to you. You have no investment in this. It was merely a spontaneous act in choosing me. It has been interesting listening to me express a position, but the truth is just that. I was watching a documentary about the Belle Knox story. The young woman went to Duke University and did porn to pay her tuition. She was outed and had since almost regretted it. She said that when she showed up for a shoot, her agent didn't tell her that she would be having sex with an older man. When she did, she said she was nearly in tears. It was not something she wanted to do. I think this is what this is. There are certain lines drawn in the sand one cannot cross. You never considered meeting me, and I knew it wasn't correct. There is maturity in knowing that. If you don't listen and your trust instincts, you face ruin."

"I will show you the draft," Frank said. "I have to orchestrate it so that it continues to tell the outside influence as well. I hope you may want to add something, like how certain correspondences made you feel, what they made you think as you read them. I am still not sure how I am going to do this. I want it to be well-edited. I love *The New Yorker* for that; it is ethereal in its ability to communicate because there is no noise in the communication, only the importance."